Babes in Toyland

Illustrated by
Erin McGonigle Brammer

Based on the original operetta by
Victor Herbert and Glen MacDonough

Ideals Children's Books • Nashville, Tennessee
an imprint of Hambleton-Hill Publishing, Inc.

For my family, friends and especially for David.
—E. M. B.

Published by Ideals Children's Books
An imprint of Hambleton-Hill Publishing, Inc.
Nashville, Tennessee 37218

Printed and bound in Mexico

Library of Congress Cataloging-in-Publication Data
Babes in Toyland / based upon the original operetta by Victor Herbert ;
    illustrated by Erin McGonigle Brammer. — 1st ed.
        p.   cm.
    Summary: A retelling, based on the 1903 operetta, of the classic
story of how two children from Mother Goose Land are pursued into
the magical Toyland by an evil uncle who wants to kill them for
their fortune.
    ISBN 1-57102-118-3
    [1. Fantasy. 2. Characters in literature—Fiction. 3. Operas—
Stories, plots, etc. 4. Toys—Fiction.] I. Herbert, Victor,
1859–1924. Babes in Toyland. II. Brammer, Erin McGonigle, ill.
PZ7.B1255   1997
[Fic]—dc21   97-5346
                                                                CIP
                                                                 AC

The illustrations in this book were rendered in oil wash, dyes, and colored pencil.
The text type is set in Goudy and Goudy Italic.
The display type is set in Biorst.

10 9 8 7 6 5 4 3 2

When you've grown up, my dears,
and are as old as I,
you'll often ponder on the years,
that roll so swiftly by.
And of the many lands
you will have journeyed through,
you'll oft recall the best of all,
the land your childhood knew!

Toyland! Toyland!
Little girl and boy land.
While you dwell within it,
you are ever happy then.
Childhood's Joyland,
Mystic, merry Toyland!
Once you pass its borders,
you can ne'er return again.

One bright, sunny morning, in the garden of Contrary Mary, the young people of Mother Goose Land gathered for a party. Soon, a lively game of tag was under way. Jack was just about to tag Little Bo Peep when a miserly looking old man strode into the garden, his cane tapping hollowly along the path.

"Jack! Jill! And dear Little Bo Peep!" he said with a chilly, crooked smile. "I hope you are all enjoying yourselves."

"We were until you came along, Barnaby," mumbled Jack.

"But I'm giving this party for you," Barnaby whined, "so that perhaps you will all be a little fonder of me."

"*You* are giving this party?" Jill asked, her eyes widening with surprise.

"No wonder the lemonade is so sour," laughed Jack.

"—and the cake so stale!" said Bo Peep. Then she added, "Why, it was only yesterday that Barnaby seized Old Mother Hubbard's shoe and turned them all out in the streets—just because she was a little late with her payments!"

"And now he's going to do the same thing to us!" wailed Jill.

"Oh no," said Barnaby, patting the girl's shoulder. "I'm going to give that cottage to your mother, the dear Widow Piper."

"Give it to her?" they all cried in disbelief.

"Yes, just as soon as Contrary Mary and I are wed."

"Ha!" scoffed Red Riding Hood. "Mary would never have you for a husband."

"Imagine! Marrying a man who never laughs!" said Jill.

"Come on!" said Jack. "Let's duck Barnaby in his own lemonade."

The youngsters cheered and gathered around Barnaby. Just as they were about to drop the old miser into the lemonade barrel, Tom-Tom, the Widow Piper's eldest son, walked into the garden.

"Tom-Tom!" shrieked Barnaby. "Don't let them drop me into my own lemonade!"

"That will hardly sweeten it!" laughed Tom-Tom as he shooed the others back to their games.

Straightening his coat, Barnaby huffed, "You really shouldn't let them treat your future brother-in-law that way!"

Tom-Tom looked at Barnaby with surprise. "Which of my sisters has caught your miserly eye?" he asked.

"The exasperating, lovable Contrary Mary!" sighed Barnaby.

"Mary! But Barnaby, you know that she's pledged to marry your nephew, Alan, just as your niece, Jane, is pledged to me."

"Nevertheless, Mary will be my bride," said Barnaby stubbornly, "just as soon as her mother and I convince her that *I* am the man she must marry."

"And how do you plan to do that?"

"It's really quite simple," Barnaby boasted. "The Widow Piper has not kept up the payments on her cottage. If Mary doesn't agree to be my wife, then I'll have no choice but to throw you all out."

"You miserly, old robber!" Tom-Tom shouted. "Get out! Get out!"

Barnaby hurried toward the gate. But before he disappeared, he turned and shook his fist at Tom-Tom, saying, "I offered you my friendship and in return you torment me! I'll get even with you—all of you!" Then he stormed out of the garden.

After Barnaby had left, Tom-Tom turned to Jill and said, "You don't really think Contrary Mary will agree to be Barnaby's bride, do you?"

"Of course not," said Jill. "At least not if she can help it."

"Where is Mary now?" asked Tom-Tom.

"She's out looking for Bo Peep's sheep."

"I have to warn her," Tom-Tom said grimly. "If I can't find Mary, I'll go to Toyland to see the Master Toymaker. Tell Mary to meet me there. The Master Toymaker was Father's dearest friend, and I'm sure that he will help us."

And with that, Tom-Tom hurried off to find his sister.

A little while later, as Jill was sweeping up the last bits of the party, Jane and Alan came into the garden. Orphaned as young children, Jane and Alan—and their inheritance—were now under the care of their uncle, old Barnaby himself.

"Is the party over already?" Jane asked.

"Yes," said Jill sadly. "It ended early because your Uncle Barnaby came in with some terrible news."

Then Jill explained all about Barnaby's plan to force Contrary Mary to be his bride. She also told them about Tom-Tom's plan to find Mary and run away to Toyland.

"Then we've got to find them!" cried Alan. "Perhaps together we can find a way to stop Uncle Barnaby." With that, Alan and Jane raced out of the garden to search for Tom-Tom and Mary.

Later that same morning, on the other side of Mother Goose Land, Mary had at last found Bo Peep's sheep. She herded them into their pen and then, knowing nothing of Barnaby's plans, she turned toward home. Finding the party over and her garden empty, Mary wandered happily among her flowers. She was busily tending to some weeds when Barnaby himself appeared, his arms filled with roses.

"For you, my dear," he said, offering Mary the roses. "Flowers to bring a smile to your lovely eyes."

Mary turned away and said matter-of-factly, "I'll grow my own flowers, thank you."

"My dear Mary, as contrary as ever I see. But I shall win you yet," chuckled Barnaby. "There's a note for you inside this bouquet, and I think it will make you quite happy."

"Don't play games, Barnaby. Just tell me what it says," replied Mary impatiently.

With some difficulty, Barnaby knelt down on one knee and said, "Marry me. I know the bloom is no longer in my cheeks, but your mother favors our marriage. Be my bride, and you shall want for nothing."

"Nothing except happiness!" cried Mary. "You know my heart belongs to Alan. Now go away and leave me alone!" Then she snatched up Barnaby's roses and threw them to the ground.

Just then, the Widow Piper came into the garden. She hurried over to her daughter. "What are you doing, Mary? Think of Barnaby's money."

"I think only of what my heart says," said Mary stubbornly.

"But imagine all that you could have. Jewels! Beautiful clothes! A golden coach! A castle to live in! Do you want us to lose our home like Old Mother Hubbard?"

"If Barnaby is that cruel, then let him turn us out in the streets," sobbed Mary, as she ran away to the far corner of her garden.

Turning to Barnaby, the Widow Piper said, "I'm sorry, Barnaby. You must overlook her contrary ways. I'll make sure she changes her mind."

"See that you do," Barnaby threatened, his wrinkled face reddening with anger, "or you'll find yourself without a roof over your head!"

"I'll do as you wish. You just keep your part of the bargain," replied the Widow Piper. Then she stepped inside the cottage and closed the door.

Some time later, Mary was still wandering through her garden, trying to find some comfort among her flowers. As she desperately wondered what to do, Alan came running up to her.

"Mary, I've been searching for you everywhere," he said, trying to catch his breath. "Tell me that nothing has changed. Tell me that you still belong to me."

Mary's eyes filled with tears, and she whispered, "Of course I do, Alan. Nothing has changed between us."

"I'm so glad," said Alan. Then, spotting Barnaby's bouquet on the ground nearby, he asked, "Who are these flowers for?" Before Mary could answer, Alan picked up the note and read aloud, "To my darling Mary. From your future . . . *husband!*"

"Alan, it's not what you think . . ."

"This is Uncle Barnaby's handwriting! To think that you could be won over by his gold!"

"It isn't so! And you're horrid to believe it!" Mary cried. "Don't ever speak to me again." Then she hurried inside the cottage, slamming the door behind her.

Alan was turning to leave the garden just as Jane came hurrying into it.

"I couldn't find Tom-Tom anywhere," she said. "He must have already left for Toyland." Then seeing the sadness on her brother's face, she asked, "What's wrong? Is it Mary?"

"Don't say her name to me ever again. She has decided to marry Uncle Barnaby."

"Uncle Barnaby!" said Jane in amazement. "Then it's his money she's after, and she's welcome to it!"

"Except for our inheritance," added Alan. "Let's go find Uncle Barnaby and demand that he give us our money."

When Alan and Jane finally found their Uncle Barnaby, he did not seem happy to see them.

"I . . . I suppose you've heard about my wedding plans," Barnaby stammered.

"That's not why we're here," snapped Alan.

"We want the money our parents left us," demanded Jane.

"Of course. I've just been keeping it safe for you. It may take time . . ."

"Now, Uncle Barnaby!" insisted Alan.

"Very well," Barnaby agreed. "I have the money hidden in a safe place, just inside the Spider Forest. I'll take you there myself."

Jane shuddered. "But the Spider Forest is full of spiders. And it's said that people who go in there never find their way out."

"Nonsense," scoffed Barnaby. "I know a path that is perfectly safe."

Reluctantly, Jane and Alan agreed to follow Barnaby. As they entered the Spider Forest, darkness seemed to close all around them. The trees grew so tall and so thick that they blocked out the sun's light, making the day seem like night. Horrible spiders perched on the sticky webs that seemed to stretch across every tree.

As the travelers reached the deepest part of the forest, Barnaby suddenly stuck out his cane. In the darkness, Jane stumbled over it and fell. She tried to stand, but could not.

"Oh, my dear Jane!" said Barnaby, pretending to be concerned. "You've twisted your ankle. You mustn't walk on it. Why don't you wait here with Alan while I go and get your money. As soon as I get back, Alan and I will carry you back to Mother Goose Land."

Before Alan or Jane could protest, Barnaby hurried off into the forest.

Hours later Barnaby had not returned. Worse still, the darkness had deepened and strange, glowing eyes had appeared to stare at them from behind the trees.

"We've got to get out of here," said Jane, glancing nervously at the eyes that lurked all around them. "I don't think Uncle Barnaby is coming back."

Alan agreed. "Our money was probably never here," he scowled.

With Jane limping along as best she could, the two tried to find their way back to Mother Goose Land. But in the darkness, they quickly became lost. As they wandered about, Jane spotted a moth caught in a spider's web.

"Look," she said. "The poor thing is as badly tangled in that web as we are in these woods. Do set it free," she pleaded.

Alan gently released the moth, and it flew to the ground near them. Fluttering its wings, the moth began to glow brightly. Jane and Alan stared in amazement as the light dipped and whirled until the moth disappeared in a cloud of shimmering brightness. Slowly the light faded and before them stood a beautiful fairy queen.

She smiled at them and said, "Thank you for saving me. For your kindness, I will lead you safely out of the forest, but first you must rest."

Suddenly realizing how very tired they were, Jane and Alan sank down against a tree and slept. In the darkness, the glowing eyes closed in on the sleepers, revealing themselves to be giant spiders. The spiders tried to spin their evil webs around the pair, but the Fairy Queen called out to the good bears of the forest who came and chased the spiders away. The bears then returned to form a circle around Jane and Alan, keeping watch over them as they slept.

In the morning, the Fairy Queen woke them and said, "Come. I will take you to Toyland where you will be safe."

While Jane and Alan journeyed toward Toyland, Contrary Mary was in her room frantically packing for a journey of her own.

"Hurry, Mary!" whispered Jill. "Mother is napping and there's no sign of Barnaby. This is your chance."

"I'm hurrying," said Mary, throwing clothes into her bag. "I've got to get to Toyland so that I won't have to marry that dreadful, old Barnaby."

Jill watched tearfully as her sister closed her bag and then began to climb out the window. "I may never see you again," Jill said.

"You mustn't say that, Jill. But while I am gone, please take care of my flowers," said Mary.

"Of course," said Jill, handing Mary her things.

Mary took one long, last look at her beloved garden, then she hurried down the lane.

Just moments later, the Widow Piper woke from her nap. She went up to Mary's room to try once more to convince her daughter to marry Barnaby. But when she opened Mary's door, she found only a sobbing Jill perched on the edge of the bed. "Where's Mary?" the Widow demanded.

"She's gone!" wailed Jill. "She's run away."

"Run away!" gasped the Widow Piper. "I'll bet she has gone to Toyland. We'll lose our home if I don't find her!" Then she ran out to find Barnaby and, together, the two of them set out for Toyland to search for Mary.

Toyland is, of course, the kingdom of childhood. It is a magical place where toy soldiers march through the streets, lollipops grow on trees, and the spirit of Christmas is alive each and every day of the year.

Toyland is ruled by the Master Toymaker himself. He is a jolly, old gentleman who, at the moment, is showing two children all the wonders of his workshop.

"Choose any toy you want, and it shall be yours," laughed the Master Toymaker. Then, with his eyes twinkling merrily, he asked, "Have you children seen the Lollipop Trees, the Laughing Well, or the Maple Syrup Lake?"

"NO!" they shouted happily.

"Well, then, you must see them at once! And when you grow up you'll remember what a wonderful place Toyland is. And perhaps you'll dream of coming back here again," said the Master Toymaker. "Now, Grumio, my helper, will show you all the wonderful sights of Toyland."

After the children had left, the Master Toymaker returned to his work, but he was soon interrupted by the arrival of Jane and Alan.

After listening closely to their story, he exclaimed, "That Barnaby is a terrible fellow! You were lucky to get out of the Spider Forest alive, but you may not be so lucky the next time you see your uncle. You must stay here in Toyland where you'll be safe."

"But we've got to go home and claim our inheritance, or Uncle Barnaby will steal it!" insisted Jane.

"I'll make sure that Barnaby doesn't steal your inheritance," the Master Toymaker assured them. "Now why don't you go out and enjoy the sights of Toyland. It will take your minds off Uncle Barnaby."

Reluctantly, Jane and Alan agreed.

"Perhaps we can find Tom-Tom," said Jane hopefully.

As Jane and Alan wandered the streets of Toyland, they saw a most terrible and unexpected sight.

"Look!" cried Jane. "It's Uncle Barnaby! Here in Toyland! Hide!" They ducked behind a tree just as Barnaby passed by on his way to see the Master Toymaker.

"Now we have to leave Toyland," said Alan. "But how will we get past Barnaby?"

Jane thought a moment and then said, "There was a company of toy soldiers in the back of the workshop. If we borrow some uniforms, we can dress up as toys. Then we can sneak on board one of the ships taking toys to Mother Goose Land. No one will ever know."

"It's a crazy scheme, but it just might work!" said Alan.

Hurrying back to the workshop, Jane and Alan scrambled into the toy soldiers' uniforms. Just as they were buttoning the last buttons, Grumio came in to prepare the toy soldiers for the parade, but to his surprise the Toy Captain's uniform was missing. Searching behind a stack of boxes, he found Jane and Alan.

"Thieves!" he shouted.

"No, no! We can explain," said Alan. Then he and Jane told Grumio their story.

"That is most unfortunate," Grumio said. "But the Christmas parade is about to start, and the Toy Captain must lead the soldiers in the parade."

"If I lead the parade, will you help us leave Toyland?" asked Alan.

"Leave it to me," said Grumio. "Just meet me here after the parade."

So with Alan and Jane leading the way, the toy soldiers marched out of the workshop and through the streets of Toyland as the crowd cheered merrily. When the parade was over, Alan and Jane rushed back to the workshop. They were waiting for Grumio when, to their surprise, in walked Contrary Mary.

Upon coming to Toyland, Mary and Tom-Tom had both taken jobs at the Master Toymaker's workshop. Tom-Tom was chief engineer for the toy trains, and Mary was the designer for the dolls' clothes.

Seeing Mary, Jane and Alan froze and pretended to be toy soldiers again. Mary made her way through the workshop, inspecting each uniform. When she came to Alan, she cried out, "My, what a start you gave me! You look so much like Alan!"

Then she went on angrily, "I wish you were Alan. To think I'd give you up for that horrible, old creature Barnaby. I'll never forgive you—never, never, never!" she said, thumping him sharply on the chest with each "never."

Mary then sighed and said, "Oh, Alan, if only you'd come back and say, 'I'm sorry. I was so wrong!' Then I'd say 'I forgive you, Alan.'"

Alan then stepped forward and said, "I'm sorry. I was so wrong!"

"Alan! It *is* you!" gasped Mary.

"So now you say . . ."

"I forgive you, Alan."

Meanwhile, on the other side of the workshop, the Master Toymaker was busily checking his list when Barnaby entered.

"Are you the Master Toymaker?" Barnaby inquired.

"I am. And who are you?"

"I am known as Barnaby."

Uncle Barnaby! the Master Toymaker exclaimed to himself.

"I want you to make some toys for me," continued Barnaby.

"What kind of toys?" asked the Master Toymaker suspiciously.

"A new kind. Toys that maim, wound, and cripple!" shrieked Barnaby with evil delight, for this would be his revenge upon those nasty children of Mother Goose Land.

"Never would I do that!" shouted the Master Toymaker in horror.

"Nonsense! Just name your price," Barnaby demanded.

"I know of only one way to convince you that I will never do as you ask," said the Master Toymaker. He reached into a drawer and pulled out a set of keys. He then led Barnaby over to a large cabinet. Unlocking the door, he pulled out a flask that glowed with an eerie green light.

"What—what is that?" asked Barnaby, stepping back cautiously.

"The spirits of evil, Barnaby. I have imprisoned them in this flask. Someday, I will have captured all the evil forces in the universe. Then children will always be happy and good. This will be my greatest gift!" said the Master Toymaker joyfully.

Barnaby's eyes glimmered with a new evil plan. "Sell me the flask!" he said. "Show me how to release these evil spirits!"

The Toymaker quickly placed the flask back in the cabinet and locked the door. "That is one thing all your gold can never buy, Barnaby. Now, get out of Toyland and never come back!"

Barnaby left the workshop in a fury. "I'll just have to get that flask some other way!"

A short time later, the Master Toymaker left to check on a shipment of toys. Barnaby watched him leave, then he slipped inside the workshop and took the keys from the drawer. Unlocking the cabinet, he removed the flask of evil spirits.

"Ah! The light of the nether world shines through! Obey my commands, evil ones! Come forth!" Barnaby shouted as he removed the stopper.

Smoke poured out of the flask, swirling and spinning until it filled the entire room. There was a loud, whirring sound, followed by flashes of light, chattering voices, and hysterical laughter.

"Spirits of evil, I command you to enter these toy soldiers!"

The spirits did so, and the toy soldiers slowly turned toward Barnaby.

"It's true!" shouted Barnaby. "I've found the secret of the spell! The soldiers turn to me, their master!"

Alan, hearing all the terrible noises, rushed into the room. "Uncle Barnaby! Undo your work before it is too late! These soldiers have evil in their black hearts!"

Barnaby looked again at the toy soldiers, who were still coming toward him. "No! No! I am your master!" he shrieked. Then he turned and ran out of the workshop with the soldiers chasing after him.

Just then, the Master Toymaker returned. "What has happened here?" he asked Alan.

Then he saw the opened flask on the counter. "Someone has freed the evil spirits! Who could have . . . ? Barnaby! It must have been him!"

At that moment the toy soldiers returned and began to surround the Master Toymaker. Alan tried to defend him, but the soldiers knocked Alan to the floor. The Master Toymaker ran out of the room with the soldiers close behind him. Seconds later, Alan heard a loud crash from the other room. Struggling to his feet, he rushed to see if the Master Toymaker was all right. Alan found him slumped against the wall. The toy soldiers had disappeared, but not before casting an evil spell on the Master Toymaker so that he could neither move nor speak.

As Alan knelt over the Master Toymaker, Barnaby came rushing back into the workshop, bringing the Toyland police with him. Pointing to Alan, Barnaby shouted, "That's him. He's the culprit. Arrest him!"

Alan looked up in surprise as the police rushed forward to arrest him.

After Alan had been led away to prison, a procession from the Palace of Justice entered the town square. The Town Crier led the procession, followed by three somber judges. Behind them were all the citizens of Toyland, as well as Barnaby, the Widow Piper, and Jane.

Unrolling a scroll, the Town Crier read, "Hear ye! Hear ye! Be it known that the Court of Justice finds Alan, the nephew of Barnaby, guilty of freeing the spirits of evil upon our fair land, so that our first citizen, the Master Toymaker, is plunged into a deep and endless sleep. And for this crime, Alan shall be banished forever to the Spider Forest."

"No, you can't do that!" cried Jane. "Alan isn't guilty!"

Barnaby turned to Jane and hissed, "Hush! You've heard the verdict of these wise and merciful judges."

"Leave Jane alone, Barnaby," said a familiar voice.

Turning, Jane saw her beloved Tom-Tom.

Just then, a policeman ran in and shouted, "Good people, Alan has escaped! He climbed over the wall and ran into the streets not ten minutes ago!"

Jane and Tom-Tom cheered.

Barnaby motioned to the crowd, "Come on. We'll capture the criminal before he escapes from Toyland."

Barnaby and the others rushed off to find Alan, leaving only Jane and Tom-Tom behind.

"Tom-Tom, I'm so glad you found me. Alan and I were going to stow away in a cargo of toys," said Jane.

"Perhaps we can still get Alan out that way," said Tom-Tom.

"If only we could wake the Master Toymaker from his trance," sighed Jane. "He could tell everyone that Alan is innocent."

"At least we've found each other," said Tom-Tom.

Hand in hand, Jane and Tom-Tom hurried back to the workshop. There they found Alan, along with Mary and Grumio, who were hurriedly trying to patch his toy soldier uniform.

"I've been promoted from captain to general," Alan joked.

"You look like you could win a war all by yourself!" said Jane.

"I may start one when I get my hands on our dear Uncle Barnaby."

While Mary was putting the finishing touches on Alan's disguise, Barnaby slipped in unnoticed and hid behind the counter.

"Grumio, how will we get Alan to the ship?" asked Tom-Tom.

"Here's the plan. We'll hide him in this box and sneak him on board the ship leaving for Mother Goose Land," said Grumio. "But we've got to work fast!"

Grumio and Tom-Tom helped Alan into the box and fastened the lid. Then, after hoisting it on a cart, they all hurried toward the ship—all except Mary, who stayed behind to hide the traces of their escape.

Seeing that Mary was alone at last, Barnaby leaped out from behind the counter.

"Barnaby!" gasped Mary.

"My dear Contrary Mary, how are you?"

"What do you want, Barnaby?"

"A wedding, my sweet. And it's a beautiful day for one, isn't it?" cackled Barnaby.

"I will not marry you, Barnaby!"

"Oh, but you will, Mistress Mary. We'll be married at once, or . . ."

"Or what?" demanded Mary impatiently.

"Or I'll hand Alan over to the police. I know how he plans to escape," sneered Barnaby.

"You would betray your own nephew when the guilt is really your own?"

"It's my duty, my dear. He bewitched the Master Toymaker, and he has been condemned for his crime."

Mary tried to run past Barnaby, but he caught her arm and said, "You needn't try to warn him. It won't do any good."

"You beast," cried Mary. Then, realizing that she had no choice, she said sadly, "All right then, Barnaby, I'll marry you. It's the only way I can save Alan."

"I thought you would see things my way. First, we'll stop at the Toyland License Bureau to take care of the legal formalities."

Having gotten the marriage license, Barnaby and Mary were on their way to the chapel when they passed Grumio, Tom-Tom, and Jane pulling a large box behind them.

Barnaby thumped the box suspiciously, "What do you have here?"

"Christmas toys for the ship at the dock," answered Grumio nervously.

"Toys, hmm? Police!" shouted Barnaby. "Hurry! The criminal you seek is there, in that box."

Suddenly, Alan burst out of the box and jumped forward with his sword drawn. "Let no man stop me if he values his life. Come, Mary."

Barnaby crowed with wicked laughter. "You haven't heard the news, nephew. I have here the license for the wedding of Contrary Mary and myself."

"Mary, tell me he lies!" Alan pleaded.

"I'm sorry, Alan. Barnaby said he would turn you in if I didn't marry him," sobbed Mary.

"Enough!" shouted Alan. Then quietly and sadly, he said, "I have no wish to escape now. I am your prisoner."

"I'm very sorry I had to do this," said Barnaby. Turning to the crowd that had gathered, he said mournfully, "There you see my dear sister's child, yet it is my painful duty to turn him over to the police."

The crowd glared at Barnaby.

Barnaby continued, "At a time like this, one feels the need for refreshment." He reached out and took a dipper full of water from a bucket that sat on the nearby well.

"It's the water from the Laughing Well!" someone whispered.

"I can't look!" said another.

Barnaby took a deep, long drink of the water. And as he did, a most amazing thing happened. Barnaby began to laugh!

It started as a titter. Then it progressed to a chuckle and then a laugh, until finally he broke into hearty, unstoppable guffaws. Barnaby staggered about, choking on his own merriment.

"Give me air! Give me air!" he gasped between fits of laughter. It was a terrible sight. The old miser laughed and laughed until he fell to the ground senseless.

Only seconds after Barnaby had fallen, the Master Toymaker appeared before the crowd.

"Hurrah!" shouted the crowd. "The charm is broken! The Master Toymaker is awakened!"

"Yes, my friends," said the Master Toymaker. "When Barnaby laughed, the spell of the evil spirits was broken. They no longer govern in Toyland, and I was released from their wicked power."

The crowd cheered again.

"But what of Barnaby?" asked Alan.

"Barnaby must receive Toyland justice for his crimes," said the Toymaker. "However, I release his intended bride to you, Alan, with my blessing."

Alan turned to Mary and said, "What say you, Mary? Is this your wish also?"

"With all my heart," she replied, smiling.

Then Tom-Tom stepped up and took the bell from the Town Crier. Ringing it loudly, he announced, "Hear ye! Hear ye! Jane, niece of Barnaby, is to wed Tom-Tom, son of the Widow Piper." Then he turned to Jane and said, "There, that makes it official."

"And so we bid farewell to strife!" declared the Master Toymaker. "Let happiness reign in Toyland forever!"